This igloo book
belongs to:

....

igloobooks

Published in 2020
by Igloo Books Ltd
Cottage Farm
Sywell
NN6 0BJ
www.igloobooks.com

0920 001
2 4 6 8 10 9 7 5 3 1
ISBN 978-1-83903-312-4

Written by Stephanie Moss
Illustrated by Hannah Wood

Designed by Alex Alexandrou
Edited by Claire Mowat

Printed and manufactured in China

WANTED
Unicorn

igloobooks

Come and join the search! We haven't got much time.

This unicorn is wanted for a very naughty crime.

WANTED

MISSING!

Very friendly. Likes running, hiding and playing tricks!

I've put up
lots of posters.
I've told all of
my friends.

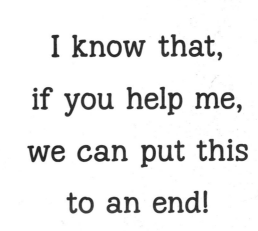

I know that,
if you help me,
we can put this
to an end!

"Please, can I have a unicorn?"

I used to always say. So when I first met Nula, it was such a happy day.

It was so unexpected when
we first came face to face.
She was out of breath, as though
she'd won a ten-mile race!

We soared into the sky on the adventure of my dreams.
It was everything I wanted, but it wasn't what it seemed.

A worldwide magic search
had started, all while we had fun.
For Nula was a criminal... and she was on the run!

At first I didn't notice
Nula acting a bit strange.

She'd been so
warm and fuzzy,
until everything changed.

She ducked behind the curtains,
even when no one was there.

She wore silly
disguises that
would hide her
rainbow hair.

But then Nula got **BORED.** That's when everything went bad.

She gave Jenny a tail when she made her really **MAD.**

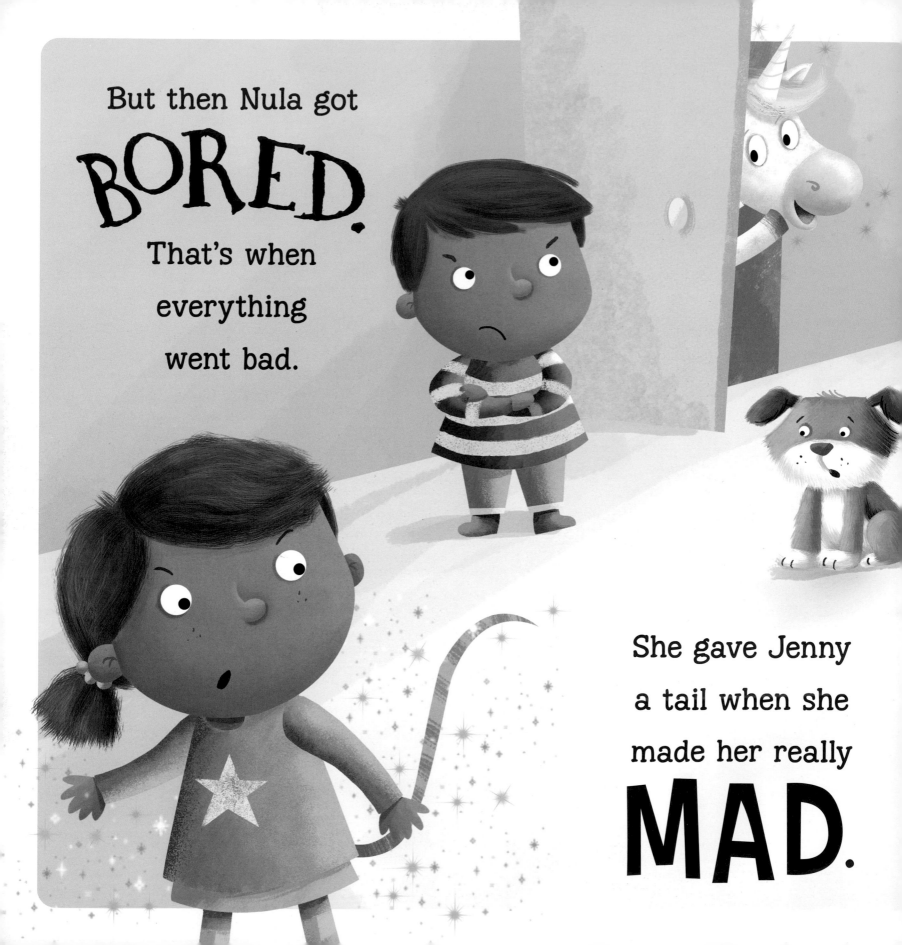

She turned
my dad into a
mouse...

... and Mum
into a **hen**.
Then she sneaked
into my school,
and guess what
happened then?

My teacher asked us all to turn our books to the next page.

Then, he was transformed into a hamster in a cage.

The class pointed and laughed. He still had a little beard!

Nula did a curtsy, and then POOF! She disappeared.

Now, I know what you're thinking.

What else had Nula done?

That's only half the story,

before she went on the run.

Was she in a gang of robbers,
stealing diamonds in the night?

Had she spray-painted graffiti
onto buildings, out of sight?

The truth is that she broke the **number one** unicorn rule.

(They teach it to all unicorns on their first day of school.)

She brought her magic
down to Earth, where we
children could see.
Now the magic squad
is after her, partly
because of me.

So, **shhh!**
Don't tell the others.
They think I'm on their side.
As I pretend to search,
I'm really helping Nula hide.

NO
UNICORNS
HERE

We tried all sorts of places, but nowhere she could stay.

For now, I'll do my best to make them look the other way.

Though Nula caused some trouble, I know her heart is good. If I were in her place, she would help me if she could.

So if you ever spot her,
wink and tell her it's okay.
I'll find her when it's safe for
her to come back out and play.